THE FANTASTIC WORLD OF THE

Oddies®

For Amber-Rose

Oddies Ltd, 1 Hay Hill, London, W1J 6DH

Text copyright © Oddies Ltd, 2003
Illustrations copyright © Oddies Ltd, 2003
Oddies is a registered trademark of Oddies Ltd
Oddieworld is a trademark of Oddies Ltd

First Published in Great Britain in 2003 by Oddies Ltd

ISBN 1-904745-02-4

Printed in Great Britain

THE STORY OF
Horsey Oddie

By Grant Slatter and Alex Hallatt

The horse rider put her favourite
pair of socks into the washing machine.

"Chug chug whirr, chug chug whirr," went the washing machine. Then it did something strange.

It speeded up really fast and there were sparkles and a tinkling sound, then a little 'pop!' Something magical had happened and one of the socks had disappeared.

The missing sock was called Horsey and she was off to Oddieworld for an adventure!

"Yaaaaay!"
she shouted as she flew past the moon.
"I can't wait to see the horses in Oddieworld."

She popped out of the Sockhole and into Oddieworld.
There, under a tree, was a very sulky looking horse.
"Hi Horsey. I need your help," said a soft voice behind her.

It was Sock Fairy.
"Lucky the horse won't go into her stable over there."

Horsey turned to look, but when she turned back
Sock Fairy had disappeared,
leaving a shiny horseshoe in her place.

"That's easy to fix," said Horsey
as she picked up the horseshoe.

"Hello," she said to Lucky.
"Look, there's your stable and I think..."
But before she could finish Wizzo rushed over.

"Don't worry," he said, "I have just the spell for this."
Then he whispered the magic words,
"Flyinus Stablus."

There was a big bang and a puff of smoke
and Wizzo shot up in the air.

He landed on Lucky, who bucked him off and then he crashed into Witchy, who was just flying past.

Horsey couldn't help but giggle!

...a big push...

..and even a tickle
behind the ears!

But Lucky wouldn't budge.
"I think I'd better go and look at your stable," said Horsey.

Cooky and Cowgirl were standing by the stable.

"Hello," said Cowgirl. "I have put down new straw and Cooky has made all sorts of delicious Horse dishes. But Lucky just won't go into her stable."

Horsey couldn't think of anything else to do and looked at her horseshoe. "I thought these were supposed to bring good luck," she said as she flipped it up in the air.

Suddenly she saw something. "That's it!" said Horsey. "The letter 'U' is missing from your name above the door, so you didn't think it was your stable any more!"

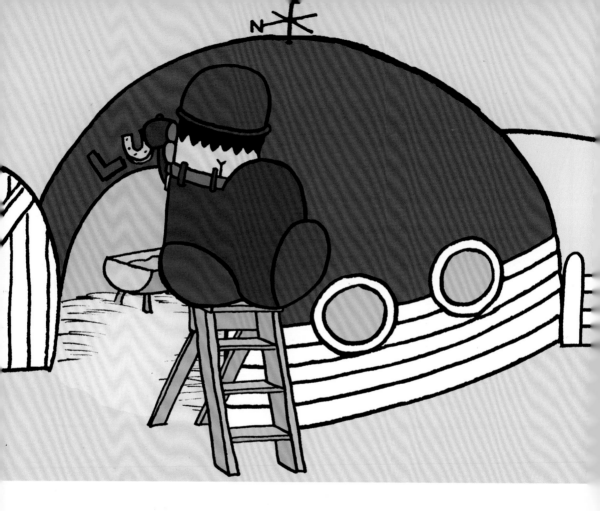

Cowgirl fetched Billy the Builder Oddie.

He fixed the horseshoe up in place of the missing letter.

Lucky the horse took one look and walked into the stable. "That horseshoe was lucky for you and lucky for Lucky!" laughed Cooky.

"Horseshoes are always lucky," said a familiar voice.

It was Sock Fairy. "We'd love you to stay in Oddieworld forever," she said, "but I'll magic you back if you really want me to." And what do you think Horsey did?

She chose to go back. "I have to go back to help
look after my own horse," she explained.
"But can I take Lucky for a ride first, please?"

Horsey rode all the way to Fairy's cottage,
round the magic lake and back to Darn Farm.

Lucky had to jump over two streams!

When it was time to go home, Sock Fairy made a magic Sock Hole appear. "Goodbye," said Horsey, "I'll come back to see you again."

Then she jumped in!

The washing machine made a tinkling sound
and a little 'pop!'

Horsey was back home.

CUT OUT AND COLOUR IN

THE FANTASTIC WORLD OF THE
Oddies®

CUT OUT AND COLOUR IN

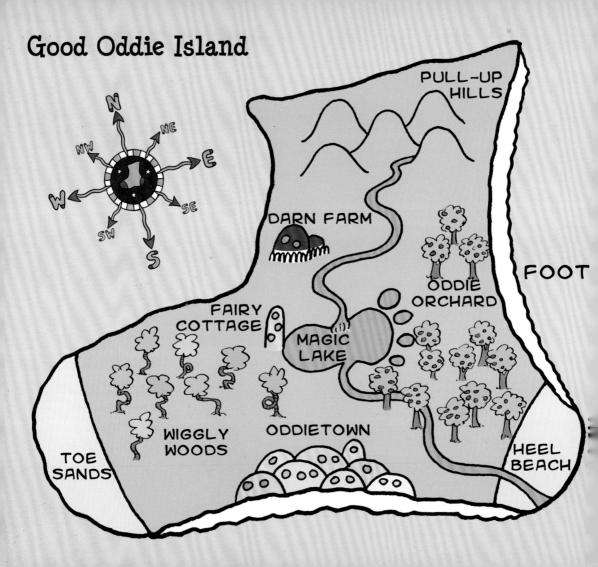